For Franky
Happy Birthday
1992
love from
K.C. & Kyle

Whisper from the Woods

Whisper from the Woods

By
Victoria Wirth

Illustrations by
A. Scott Banfill

GREEN TIGER PRESS

Published by Simon & Schuster

New York · London · Toronto · Sydney · Tokyo · Singapore

GREEN TIGER PRESS
Simon & Schuster Building, Rockefeller Center
1230 Avenue of the Americas, New York, New York 10020
Text copyright © 1991 by Victoria Wirth
Illustrations copyright © 1991 by A. Scott Banfill
All rights reserved including the right
of reproduction in whole or in part in any form.
GREEN TIGER PRESS is an imprint of
Simon & Schuster Inc.
Manufactured in Hong Kong.
10 9 8 7 6 5 4 3 2 1

Library of Congress Cataloging-in-Publication Data
Wirth, Victoria.
Whisper from the Woods/by Victoria Wirth:
illustrated by A. Scott Banfill. p. cm.
Summary: A poetic portrayal of the cycle of life of a
forest as they share thoughts and wisdom over the years.
[1. Forests—Fiction. 2. Trees—Fiction.]
I. Banfill, A. Scott, ill.   II. Title.
PZ7.W7746Wh 1991 [Fic]—dc20
ISBN: 0-671-74790-8

To Sarah Rains, with love
—Victoria Wirth

To Mom and Dad—A. Scott Banfill

In the darkness of the forest,
in a quiet unlit corner, a
seed fell from the branch of
a very old tree.

It landed on the green
moss and rolled into a dip
in the soft ground.

There it began to grow.

When the old tree looked
down and saw the tiny
seedling below, she moved
her branches ever so slowly
aside, and a tiny ray of light
slipped to the bottom of
the dim forest floor.

The seedling reached up
to touch the light with
small pale leaves...

Then he grew and grew.

As time went on, other
seeds fell and began to grow.
Each time, the old tree
moved her branches so that
they too might grow up
beside her.

Year passed year and they
grew tall, straight,
and strong.

All day long in warm
summer breezes these trees,
young and old, would
lean together and whisper;
sharing thoughts and
passing the wisdom of
many years.

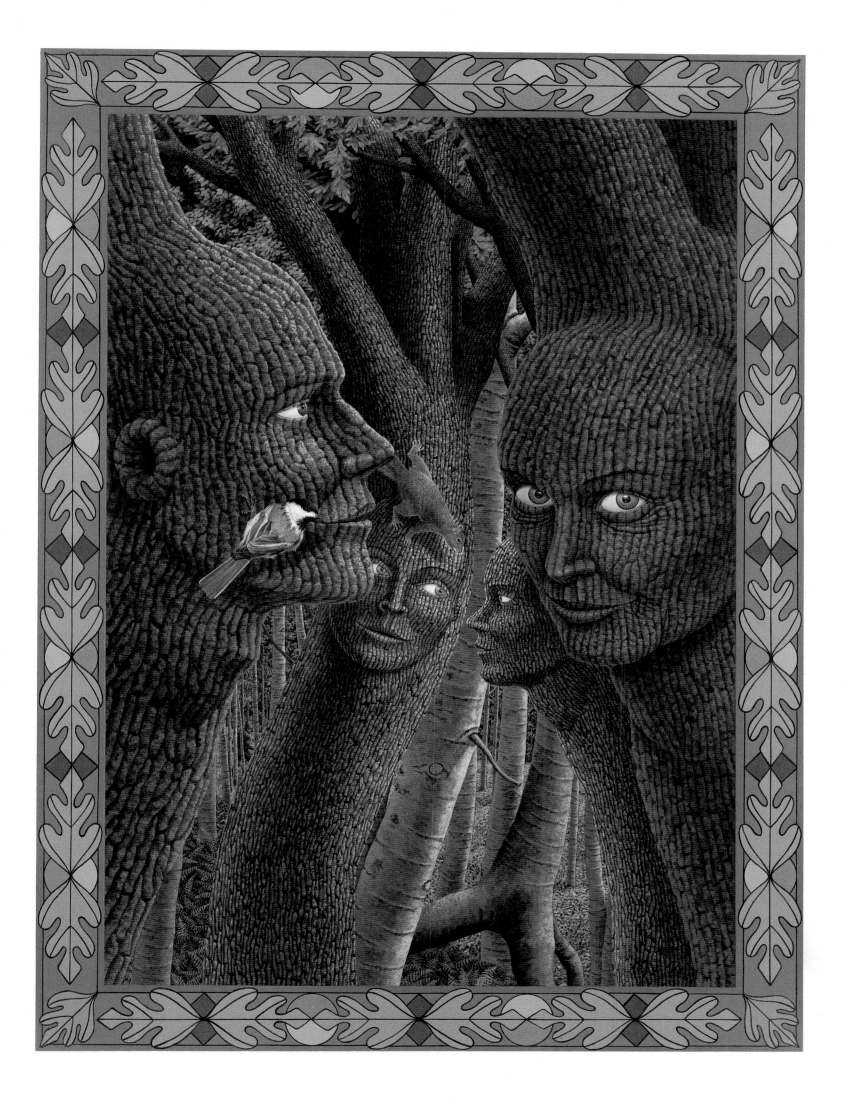

In winter, asleep they'd
stand, hand reached hand,
roots gently touched
underground.

One day the old tree
sighed and that night in
a terrible storm...

She fell and leaned against
the first seedling.

And the branch that held
her was steady and strong.

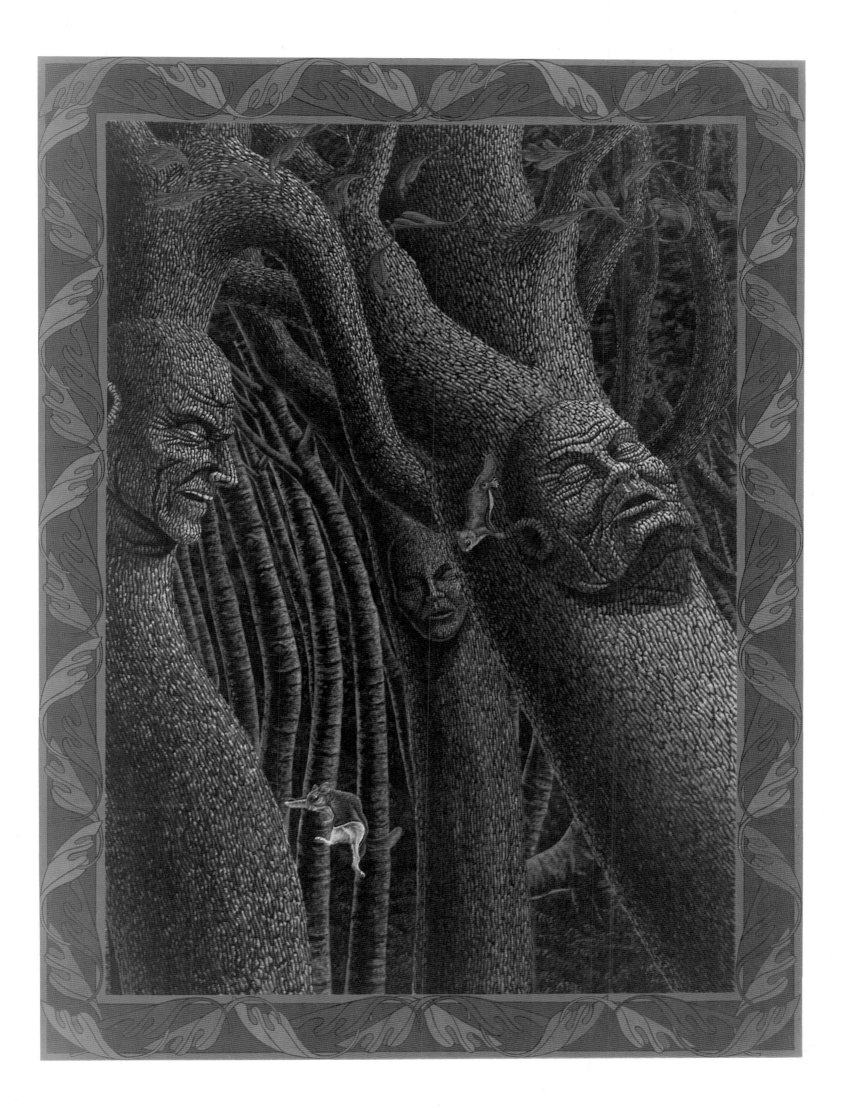

When the rains came the
old tree slipped quietly to
the ground at the feet of those
young trees—her children.
They covered her with their
leaves and sheltered her
from the storms.

In the spring the first
seedling dropped a seed
to the forest floor. It
rolled into a dip in the soft
ground and there
began to grow.

A. Scott Banfill's paintings were done in acrylics.
The dimensions of the originals are 17″ by 23.″
The text of this book is set in Tiepolo by
Andresen Typographics, L.A., Calif.
Design by Judythe Sieck.